Bill is No Bully

Written and Illustrated

By

Cindy Hedeman

Best Wishes,
Cindy Hedeman

This book is dedicated to my husband, Gary "Roach" Hedeman, who asked me to write "A little story about Bill," and my sister in law Cheryl, who strongly suggested I illustrate this book myself.

Bill was born on a crisp spring morning on the Bradford Ranch in Texas. His arrival was much awaited by his owner, Alexis, for he was destined to be a famous bucking bull, like many of his relatives and fellow ranch tenants. Many of the herd, cows and bulls came to peer upon the Charlais calf.

As Bill grew and grew, he tried to join in the bucking bull games like, "Hook the Cowboy". His heart just wasn't in it.

He found himself wanting to visit with the other ranch inhabitants like the ranch dog, cat, and horse. He would talk to them about all kinds of things, the weather, or who was the favorite ranch hand. Things that the other bulls thought were unimportant. Bill just wanted to make friends.

The other young bucking bulls made fun of Bill and called him names like "Cowboy Lover" and "Rancher's Pet." Bill knew the best thing was not to react. So he ignored them.

The herd bulls got wind of Bill's new friends and decided to have a talk with him. They surrounded Bill and his friends.

Being surrounded by the bullies made Bill nervous. He knew he should stay with his friends and look to the rancher for help.

Red Rocket tried to hook, Bristow, the blue heeler. Bill stepped in front of Bristow blocking Red Rocket to protect his friend.

Mean Machine snorted and exclaimed, "You are not acting like a bucking bull! Bucking bulls are mean, nasty, and hook dogs and cowboys!"

Bill really was afraid but he knew it would be wrong to try to be something he wasn't. He knew he should respond to the bullies with factual information.

So he took a deep breath and faced the angry bulls. He said," I'm sorry you don't like who I am, but I will not act like you want me to. It's a shame you feel threatened by me because I don't fit in, but you don't have to be mean to be a good bucking bull."

"Yes, you do!" shouted the bullies.

"Look at *Corpus Red* and *Barbedwire*", countered Bill. "They like their owner to scratch them on their heads!

Bill continued, "The famous Bad Company bull, *Party Animal*, used to buck guys off, then stop, and allow himself to be led with a halter to take pictures with kids!

"No way!" the bullies shouted.

Bill added, "The PRCA Bucking Bull of the year, *Biloxi Blues,* had a cousin that let his owner feed him a cow cube from his mouth."

"Say it isn't so!" cried Red Rocket, the leader of the bull gang.

"It's the truth," said Bill, "and I won't stand by and watch you bully my friends because you're not educated." Bill turned to Rancher Joe who was already on his way to corral the bullies.

The bulls snorted, pawed the ground, and backed up.

After a long pause and shaking of their heads, the bulls looked at each other and felt ashamed.

They decided that they should all be more like Bill.

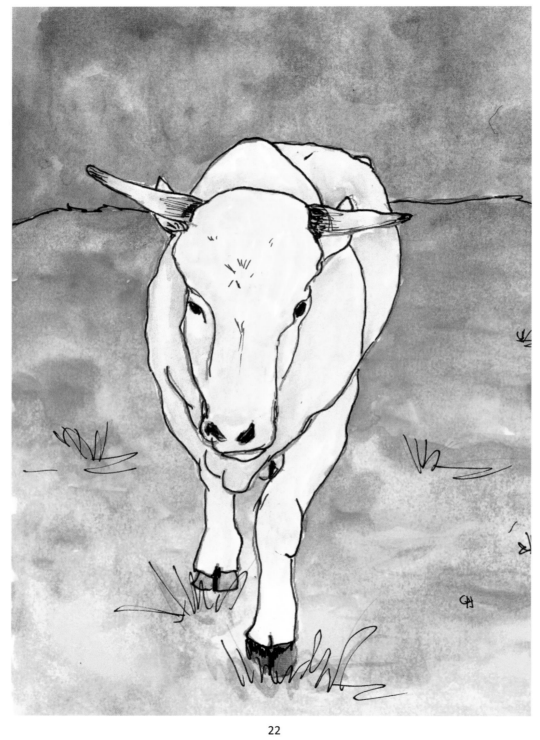

About the Author

Cindy Hedeman resides in Bowie, Texas with her family. She has been a professional educator for over 30 years. She enjoys teaching art, technology, and working with her gifted students. Her experiences in the education field have made her aware of many problems students face today which inspired her to write , *Bill is No Bully*. Her hobbies include drawing, painting, and barrel racing.

Author's Notes

- Many of the characters in this story are based on real animals.

- Pg. 10 Red Rocket is a real bucking bull currently performing at professional bull ridings.

- Pg. 15 Corpus Red is a real superstar in the bucking bull world. He is often a short go or bounty bull for the CBR.

- Pg. 16 This illustration was done from a photograph of former PRCA and PBR bullfighter Roach Hedeman and daughter Katie, with real Party Animal.

- Pg. 17 "Roach the Bull" did eat cow cake from my husband's mouth. He was owned by us and trained by George Haynes.

- Pg. 22 Bill resides with us in Bowie, TX. He is owned by Alexis Bradford.